The ALIEN HUNTER'S GUIDE

Gomer Bolstrood

SEA-TO-SEA

Mankato, Collingwood, London

On a warm summer night, nothing beats lying in the cool grass gazing up at the stars. You might even notice lights in the sky, like shooting stars or paper lanterns people have let loose into the night air. Or are they? What if they turn out to be UFOs—the craft of alien visitors?

This book shows you how to tell alien craft from fakes (or mistakes), using examples of famous alien encounters. It identifies the types of alien that people have reported encountering most often, and gives some ideas for what to do if you DO happen to bump into one!

Good luck!

Gomer Bolstrood

CONTENTS

4   UFOS EVERYWHERE!

6   FOO FIGHTERS

8   THE FLATWOODS MONSTER

10   THE OHIO UFO

12   THE NULLARBOR PLAINS UFO

14   THE BELGIAN UFO WAVE

16   MEXICAN UFO WAVE

18   AREA 51

20   THE WESTENDORFF UFO

22   THE ILLINOIS UFO

24   CHINA'S UFO CRAZE

26   ALIENS ON SCREEN

28   TYPES OF ALIEN

30   TECHNICAL INFORMATION

31   MORE UFO & ALIEN INFORMATION

32   INDEX

Words in **bold** are in the glossary

UFOS Everywhere!

What *is* that strange light outside your window at night? It could just be a passing car…but what if it's not? What if it's actually something far more mysterious? What if it's actually a UFO, piloted by aliens?

UFO Alert

UFO stands for "unidentified flying object" so, technically, a UFO is anything flying that you don't recognize. But that is not what people usually mean when they talk about UFOs. They mean craft piloted by aliens, or visitors from outer space. Ever since ancient times, people have seen these mysterious ships in the sky, usually at night. Sometimes they even encounter the UFO's pilots.

Crackpots and Counterfeits

Claiming to have seen a UFO is a great way to get attention. There a lot of people out there who have faked UFO and alien sightings for fame or money. So a dedicated alien hunter needs to be ready to put sightings into one of two main categories: Case Open, Fake or Mistake.

◀ *A faint, blurry object in the evening sky. Could it be an alien craft?*

Alien Hunter's Toolkit

Any good alien hunter will always have the following in his or her toolkit:

• Camera for visual evidence.

• Voice recorder to record what witnesses say.

• Writing pad for making sketches and notes.

• Small, sealed holders for soil and plant samples from the landing site.

Some hunters also use a Geiger counter, a device that measures **radiation** levels. High radiation levels could indicate a UFO visit.

FANTASTIC SIGHTS LEAP AT YOU

IN **3-DIMENSION**

AMAZING!
EXCITING!
SPECTACULAR!

IT

CAME FROM OUTER SPACE

From Ray Bradbury's great science fiction story!

Starring
Richard CARLSON · Barbara RUSH
WITH CHARLES DRAKE · RUSSELL JOHNSON
KATHLEEN HUGHES · JOE SAWYER

◄ *People have long believed in the existence of aliens from outer space, as this movie poster and speech from the 1950s show.* ▼

"The nations of the world will have to unite, for the next war will be an interplanetary war. The nations of the Earth must someday make a common front against attack by people from other planets."

- General Douglas MacArthur, speaking in 1955.

Foo Fighters

Alien Fact File

Name: Foo fighters
Location: Europe, Pacific Ocean
Sighted: 1st official report
November 1944

Foo fighters became famous as the first modern UFOs. They are small, fast-moving balls of bright light, anything from a few inches to more than a yard across. No one has ever been able to figure out for sure where foo fighters come from.

▼ A foo fighter suddenly appears close to a bomber plane.

▲ This photo is said to show a foo fighter. It was taken by a German pilot flying over Germany in May 1945.

The Foo Fighters Appear

Foo fighters first appeared during nighttime bombing raids in World War II (1939–1945). They began following military aircraft through the sky, darting around at speeds of up to 500 mph (800km/h). They did not appear on radar screens, but were clearly visible to aircrews. Although foo fighters never attacked a plane, some pilots reported that their instruments, and even their engines, failed when foo fighters came close to them.

A New Weapon?

Ar first, the **Allies** thought the foo fighters might be a new, secret enemy weapon. But it emerged after the war that foo fighters had also targeted German and Japanese pilots. Many people began to think that the fighters must be some kind of alien technology.

Over the years, secret official documents have been released showing that the foo fighters did exist. But despite more than 50 years of investigation, there has never been a definite explanation of what the foo fighters are.

CASE OPEN
Further investigation needed

The Flatwoods Monster

Alien Fact File

Name: Flatwoods Monster;
Phantom of Flatwoods
Location: West Virginia
Sighted: September 12, 1952

Imagine seeing a ball of fire blaze across the evening sky, then crash behind some hills. A group of local kids go to investigate. They come back claiming that a gigantic, hissing alien has confronted them. That's exactly what happened one evening in 1952, in the town of Flatwoods, West Virginia.

The Monster's Appearance

The Flatwoods Monster was said to be at least 10 feet (3m) tall, with a glowing red face. It was hooded and had bulging eyes. Its body was **humanoid**, and it wore a dark green cloak. Its arms ended in long, clawed fingers and, apparently, it released a strange mist.

UFOs had been spotted right across the U.S. that day, including above the capital, Washington, DC. People were puzzled and fearful. Could the strange aircraft be piloted by enemies of the U.S. from outer space? Was this, in fact, the start of an alien invasion?

▲ An artist's impression of the famous Flatwoods Monster.

8

> "Skid marks were found near the hill, and a depressed circle in the grass, entirely like the marking that might be made if a large object had 'parked' there...."
>
> – An eyewitness description of the crash site.

UFO—or Meteor?

Alien hunters soon discovered that a **meteor** had been seen that night in the skies above Maryland, Pennsylvania, and West Virginia. In other locations the meteor had mistakenly been reported as a blazing aircraft crashing to the ground. It seemed likely that the Flatwoods UFO-spotters had made the same error, while the monster may have simply been an animal, such as a large owl!

▲ It would be easy to convince yourself that a meteor like the one above was an alien craft.

FAKE OR MISTAKE!
Not a UFO/Alien

The Ohio UFO

Alien Fact File

Name: The Ohio UFO
Location: Ohio and Pennsylvania
Sighted: April 17, 1966

The Ohio UFO sightings in April 1966 became famous around the world. Witnesses included several police officers. The UFO became so famous that it inspired one of the most successful alien movies of all time, Steven Spielberg's *Close Encounters of the Third Kind*.

Dawn Patrol

Events began just before dawn on April 17, 1966. Two police officers got out of their patrol car to investigate an abandoned vehicle at the side of the road. As they stood there, a low-flying UFO rose up out of the trees, lighting up the area "like it was Christmas." The UFO was shaped like a wide ice-cream cone, and made a loud humming noise.

High-Speed Pursuit

The police officers ran to their car and radioed in a report. They were told to follow the UFO if it moved off. In the end, the police followed the alien craft nearly 85 miles (135km) into the neighboring state of Pennsylvania. Along the way, more police joined in the pursuit.

▶ *Many motorists reported being overtaken by the Ohio UFO.*

▲ *This scene is from the movie* Close Encounters of the Third Kind, *which was inspired by the events in Ohio.*

The UFO Departs

Near the town of Conway, Pennsylvania, the UFO stopped moving. As the police officers watched it, they heard radio reports that fighter jets were being scrambled to investigate the UFO. Then, in the words of Deputy Sheriff Dale Spaur:

"When they started talking about fighter planes, it was just as if that thing heard every word that was said. It went PSSSSSHHEW, straight up. And I mean when it went up, friend, it didn't play no games— it went straight up."

ALIEN ENCOUNTERS

Encounters with aliens are categorized into three basic types:

• **Close encounters of the first kind:**

Sighting of a UFO.

• **Close encounters of the second kind:**

Sighting of a UFO, sensing heat or radiation traces, evidence of a landing site, **lost time,** or effects on engines, electrical items, etc.

• **Close encounters of the third kind:**

Sighting or contact with living creatures associated with UFOs, presumed to have come from it.

THE NULLarbor PLains UFO

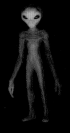

Imagine driving along a lonely road late at night, when suddenly a bright light appears. Your car starts behaving strangely as the light gets closer and closer. However fast you go, you cannot shake it—a UFO has you in its sights. That's just what happened to Faye Knowles and her three sons one night in 1988.

▼ *As the UFO approached, Faye Knowles's car engine started cutting out, and its electrical systems began to flicker and fade.*

Alien Fact File

Name: Nullarbor UFO
Location: South Australia/ Western Australia
Sighted: January 19, 1988

A Lonely Road

The Knowles family was driving along the Eyre Highway, crossing the Nullarbor Plain. The Plain is one of Australia's bleakest deserts. There was little other traffic on the road, just a couple of trucks visible in the far distance.

The Alien Craft Appears

Suddenly, the family noticed a bright light moving at high speed, at the top of a swirling column. The UFO whizzed up, and hovered over their car. Then, terrifyingly, the car began to lift off the highway. Suddenly it crashed back down to the road, and the UFO disappeared. One tire was ruined, and the roof was dented, as if something had been clamped onto it.

A truck driver came forward and said that he had witnessed the events and that the Knowles family was telling the truth. Today, some people remain convinced that this was one of Australia's many UFO encounters. Others, though, suggest that they actually encountered an electrically charged tornado.

▼ *At night, a tornado like this one could be mistaken for a UFO's* **tractor beam.**

CASE OPEN
Further investigation needed

The Belgian UFO Wave

Alien Fact File

Name: Belgian UFO Wave, The Triangles
Location: Belgium
Sighted: First sighted November 29, 1989

Most people don't spend time looking for UFOs or aliens. But once someone has seen one, everyone's attention is drawn to the sky. Before you know it, there are reports of alien craft turning up all over the place! That's certainly what happened in Belgium between 1989 and 1990.

▼ *UFO spotters try to attract the attention of alien visitors.*

LIGHTS IN THE SKY

The first Belgian UFOs were reported in November 1989. So many people reported mysterious lights in the sky that an Air Force fighter was sent to investigate. The lights turned out to be from a local disco, but they started people thinking that there were UFOs out there.

THE CLUMSY UFO

In December 1989, there were numerous reports of an egg-shaped UFO above the Belgian cities of Namur and Liège. The UFO was not very good at flying, and at one point it got trapped in a tree,

before freeing itself and floating off into the distance. Today, this seems likely to have been the work of an eccentric inventor, conducting tests of a radio-controlled balloon.

THE TRIANGLES

The next wave of sightings happened in 1990. Many Belgians, including police officers, and the army, reported seeing triangular UFOs that became known as the "Triangles." One was even tracked by jet fighters, playing cat-and-mouse with them for over an hour before disappearing. There has never been a definite explanation of what the Triangles were.

TRIANGLE EVIDENCE

Whatever the Triangles were, there is evidence that *something* mysterious was in the skies above Belgium:
• They appeared on the radar of fighter planes.
• The Triangle the fighters chased made some amazing maneuvers, including rapidly accelerating to 1,100mph (1,770km/h), and dropping 3,000 feet (900m) in two seconds, neither of which can be done by any known aircraft.

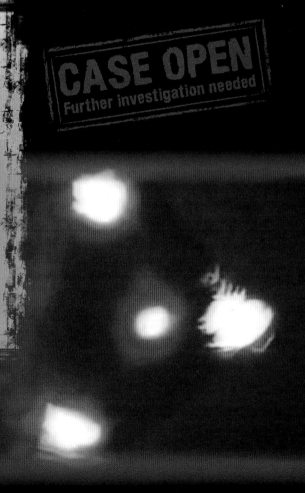

CASE OPEN
Further investigation needed

▶ This blurry photo, taken in 1990, shows one of the Belgian triangles.

MEXICAN UFO WAVE

Mexico is one of the top destinations for visiting UFOs. Soon after a sighting in 1991, the entire country became gripped by UFO fever.

Alien Fact File

Name: Mexican UFO Wave
Location: Mexico
Sighted: Sightings began April 1991

▼ *A UFO is seen from a plane in the skies above Mexico City.*

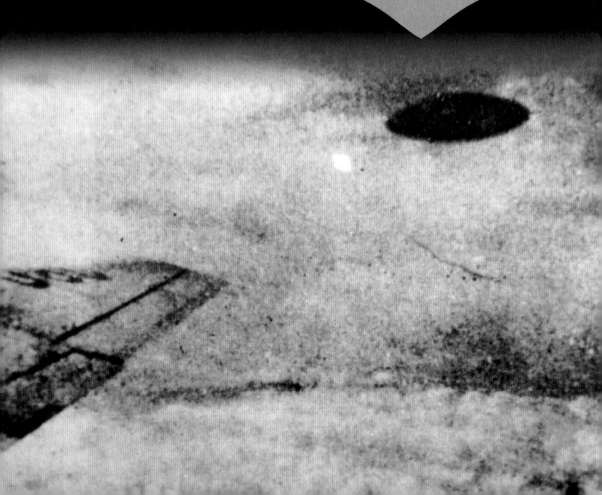

First Contact

The sightings began in April 1991, when a girl and her brothers saw a fireball in the sky. Moments later, two humanoid aliens signaled to them with a red light. The next month there were two other sightings of UFOs, and the Mexican UFO Wave had begun.

Selected Encounters

Hundreds of alien encounters were reported. Key events included:
• Sightings of triangles like those seen in Belgium (see page 15) over the city of Pachuca.
• A brilliant light, followed by an unexplained explosion, in the city of Jojutla.

• Flying saucers, a **mother ship**, and "ghost flyer" UFOs over the city of Ciudad Valle.
• People across Mexico reported encounters with small aliens, and there were reports of the military retrieving the wreckage of crashed UFOs.

Mexico's UFO Wave began to decline in the middle of the 1990s, though sightings were still reported. In the end, most people stopped believing that the UFOs were real when a famous sighting in 1997 (now known as the Las Lomas UFO **hoax**, see box below) was widely decided to be a fake.

THE LAS LOMAS UFO HOAX

On August 6, 1997, a video seemed to show a UFO in the skies above Mexico City. It quickly spread around the world (and can still be seen on the Internet). But when similar results were produced by a film crew with a tiny model and some cardboard cutouts, people began to think that the video was most likely a hoax.

FAKE OR MISTAKE! Not a UFO/Alien

MILENIO

AUG. 6 1997

▲ This is a convincing image of a UFO above Mexico City in 1997—but it's a fake.

Area 51

Far out in the Nevada desert—in an area where the map says there are no towns—is a secretive military base known as Area 51. The purpose of Area 51 has long been the subject of alien-hunter speculation.

Alien Fact File

Name: Area 51
Location: Nevada
Sighted: Area 51 has existed since at least 1967

▲ *Signs warn people not to go any farther—this trail leads toward Area 51.*

UFO Alert

Many alien hunters believe that Area 51 is where captured UFOs are taken and investigated so that their technology can be explored and then put to military use. If alien remains, or living aliens, are found, they are also taken to Area 51.

Area 51 Rumors

There are many strange rumors about what happens in Area 51. They include:
• Meetings with aliens
• Development of technology to control the weather
• Time travel and **teleportation** machines
• An underground railroad that crosses North America
• A runway that is only visible when water is sprayed onto it.

Security at Area 51

The U.S. military is reluctant to talk about what actually goes on in Area 51. It is clear that in the past, new aircraft were developed here in secret. The military tries to keep the base from prying eyes. The airspace nearby and above is restricted to prevent nonmilitary aircraft from flying overhead, and signs, security fences, cameras, and other devices ward off intruders.

ROSWELL

In Roswell, New Mexico, the wreckage of a UFO was apparently recovered in 1947, then taken away by the U.S. military. In fact, the wreckage was almost certainly from an experimental weather balloon that had crashed. Even so, some people claim that the body of at least one dead alien was also taken from the site.

CASE OPEN
Further investigation needed

▼ *A grainy image from an unidentified source that claims to show one of the Roswell aliens being experimented on.*

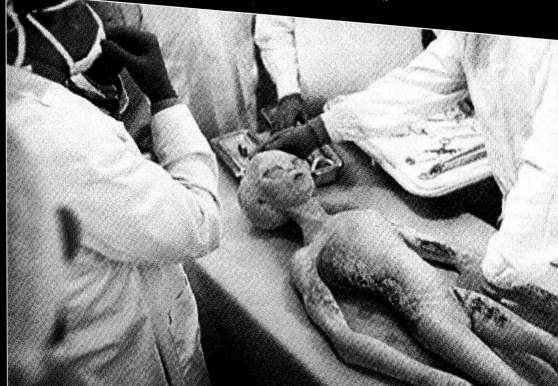

THE WESTENDORFF UFO

Alien Fact File

Name: Westendorff UFO
Location: Rio Grande do Sul, Brazil
Sighted: October 5, 1996

Flying in a small plane can be a scary experience at the best of times. Just imagine how frightening it would be to take off and then realize you were sharing the skies with a UFO the size of a football field. That's just what happened to Brazilian Haroldo Westendorff in 1996.

The UFO Appears

Westendorff had been in the air for about an hour when he caught sight of a giant UFO. After taking his tiny plane closer, he was able to give a good description of the smooth metallic alien ship:

• It was triangular in shape, about 328 feet (100m) wide and around 165–200 feet (50–60m) tall.
• On the base there were eight raised areas, each of which had three balls of some kind on it.

Independent Evidence

Westendorff asked the control tower at the nearby Pelotas airport if they could see anything in his direction. "Yes," came the reply, "a gray, triangular shape with blurry edges." The local radar station, however, could not see the UFO on its screens.

Westendorff flew around the UFO for about ten minutes. His heart almost stopped when a door opened in the side of the UFO, and a smaller UFO came flying out. It sped away toward the horizon at incredible speed, and moments later the **mother ship** flew rapidly straight up in the air. Haroldo's close encounter was over.

THE VARGINHA ALIENS

The Westendorff UFO was not the only alien craft spotted over Brazil in 1996. In the town of Varginha there was a series of sightings of UFOs, and as many as six aliens. The aliens were described as being about 5 feet (1.5m) tall, with thin bodies, large heads, and glowing red eyes. No evidence of the UFOs or aliens has ever been found.

▼ This drawing of a UFO closely resembles the huge UFO seen by Westendorff in 1996.

The ILLINOIS UFO

Alien Fact File

Name: Illinois UFO/Illinois Police
Sighting/Highland UFO
Location: Illinois
Sighted: January 4–5, 2000

On January 4, 2000, a giant UFO was spotted over Illinois. It was the size of a football field, made almost no noise, and moved so slowly that it seemed to be hovering in the air. Underneath it were rows of lights.

▼ This giant UFO spent several hours flying silently over Illinois in 2000.

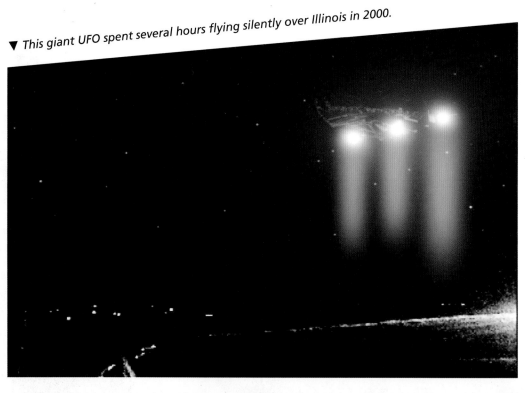

First reports of the UFO came in at about 10:30 P.M. A completely silent craft, much bigger than a jumbo jet, had appeared over the town of Forest Lake, Illinois. The craft was brightly lit underneath, where there were rows of tiny lights. The police and public spotted the UFO over the town of Lebanon, then again over the town of Shiloh. Sometimes it glided slowly while at other times it zipped off at amazing speed.

▼ Some investigators have suggested the Illinois UFO could have been a stealth aircraft like this one. However, stealth planes are not known to be able to fly silently.

Possible Explanations

Several explanations were put forward as to what was in the skies of Illinois that night:
• a runaway **blimp**
• a stealth bomber
• the planet Venus, low in the sky
• a lighter-than-air, rigid airship.

None of these would be able to make the kind of rapid changes of direction or speed the UFO made. The true nature of the UFO that hovered over Illinois in January 2000 is still not known.

CASE OPEN
Further investigation needed

"It was just a very surreal experience."

– One of the Illinois UFO witnesses.

CHINA'S UFO Craze

In late 1999 and early 2000, following thousands of sightings, China became gripped by UFO fever. More than 3,000 alien craft were reported in 1999 alone.

One of China's biggest UFO stories happened in 2002, when a UFO was spotted by hundreds of witnesses. It was orange and white, and was brightly lit. Witnesses said that it constantly changed shape. One minute it looked like a flaming arrow, the next it was cone-shaped, or looked like an open fan.

Alien Fact File

Name: Chinese UFO Craze
Location: China
Sighted: Starting late in 1999

▼ This image is said to show the alien craft that flew across China in 2002.

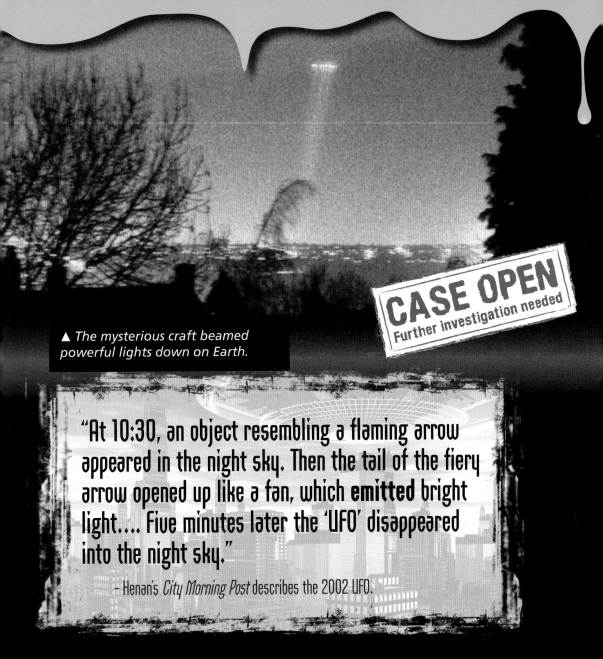

▲ *The mysterious craft beamed powerful lights down on Earth.*

"At 10:30, an object resembling a flaming arrow appeared in the night sky. Then the tail of the fiery arrow opened up like a fan, which **emitted** bright light.... Five minutes later the 'UFO' disappeared into the night sky."

– Henan's *City Morning Post* describes the 2002 UFO.

RIGHT ACROSS CHINA

The UFO crossed large areas of China, traveling swiftly from east to west. It upset wedding guests in Lin Yao, mystified a military pilot in Sichuan province, frightened fishermen on the Yangtze River, and troubled thousands of others. Alien hunters soon began to try to track down the identity of the mysterious craft.

WHAT WAS IT?

Astronomers agree something mysterious was in the sky over China that evening. They think the UFO was some sort of "3-dimensional flying machine" and that it was a real craft, not a planet, meteor, or some other natural event. They also agree that they do not know whether it was designed by humans or came from outer space.

ALIENS ON SCREEN

Aliens and UFOs have always made for good TV and movie action. People love a scary thrill, and the idea of invaders from outer space has been providing it since H.G. Wells published *The War Of The Worlds* in 1898. These are just a few of the most famous motion pictures with an alien theme.

The War Of The Worlds

H.G. Wells' book tells the tale of aliens from Mars who invade England. When it was broadcast as a radio show in 1938, it caused panic among listeners who thought a Martian invasion was really taking place! Since then, the story has also been made into TV shows and movies.

E.T. The Extra-Terrestrial

One of the most successful movies ever, *E.T.* showed that aliens weren't always interested in invading Earth and killing its people. The story tells of a young alien accidentally left behind when his UFO leaves without him. His young human friends try to help him find his way home, all while trying to stop the grownup world from interfering.

▼ E.T. and his human friend Elliott in a scene from the movie E.T.

Men in Black I and II

These comic movies tell the story of the black-suited MIB agency. MIB secretly helps aliens who have come to Earth seeking shelter, and protects them from threats from other aliens. *Men in Black III* is due out in 2012.

▶ *Will Smith as Agent J in* Men in Black I *gets to grips with a baby alien.*

"There's always an Arquillian Battle Cruiser, or a Corillian Death Ray, or an intergalactic plague that is about to wipe out all life on this miserable little planet, and the only way these people can get on with their happy lives is that they Do. Not. Know."

– Agent Z in *Men in Black.*

TYPES OF ALIEN

If they do exist, what kind of shape do our visitors from outer space usually take? They appear in a wide range of forms, from lizards to hairy beasts to little gray people.

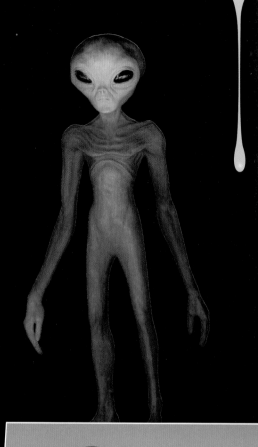

▶ *An artist's impression of a little gray alien or "Gray" (see below).*

"Gray" Visitors

Grays are short, humanoid creatures. They are known as Grays because of their grayish colored skin. They are usually reported as being about 4 feet (1.25m) tall, and have frail, thin bodies. Most Grays seem to have large heads, and big, black, almond-shaped eyes.

Animal Aliens

Many aliens with an animal-like form have been reported. Most common are aliens with a slightly **reptilian** appearance. These are closely followed by visitors resembling insects from outer space. Some aliens with qualities like birds have also been seen occasionally.

▶ *The aliens in the movie* District 9 *(see page 27) look like a cross between insects and shrimp.*

MONSTROUS ALIENS

There are other creatures associated with UFOs:
• The Flatwoods Monster—(see pages 8–9).
• The Mothman, which appeared in 1966–7, soon after a spate of UFO sightings in the area around Point Pleasant, West Virginia.
• The bloodsucking chupacabras monster, which some people claim is associated with UFO sightings in North and South America. However, when one was captured, it was found to be a coyote with a skin infection.

▲ *An artist's impression of The Mothman, which some people think is an alien.*

"You're going out there to destroy them [aliens], right? Not to study, not to bring back, but to wipe them out?"

- Ripley, the hero/alien fighter of the *Alien* movies.

Technical Information

Words from this Book:

Allies
during World War II, this described the UK, U.S., and those countries that fought alongside them.

astronomer
scientist who studies the night sky and planets.

blimp
small, nonrigid airship.

emitted
gave out or released.

hoax
a trick. Many UFO photos turn out to be hoaxes produced by people who hope to gain fame or money.

humanoid
looking similar to humans, but not human.

lost time
time that has passed without someone having any memory of it.

meteor
a piece of rock from space that burns with a bright light and leaves a trail behind it in the sky.

mother ship
a ship that provides supplies and facilities for smaller vessels.

radiation
a form of energy.

reptilian
like a reptile in appearance.

teleportation
transporting something by making it disappear and then reappear somewhere else.

tractor beam
a beam of light from a spaceship that pulls things toward it.

Alien-Hunting Tools

The basic toolkit of an alien hunter is detailed on page 7, but here are two more sophisticated tests anyone with access to a lab may be able to try:

Soil analysis—soil samples from possible UFO landing sites can be analyzed to find out if they contain unusual or unknown material. Obviously, never take soil samples from gardens, etc. without the owner's permission.

Photo analysis—in the past, UFO photos were faked by "double exposure," taking two photos on a single piece of film, one of a model UFO, the other of a convincing background. Today, the same trick can be achieved digitally. Only expert analysis can reveal whether photos are genuine or not.

More UFO & Alien Information

Other Books

*A Practical Guide To Vampires
UFOs and Aliens: Investigating
Extraterrestrial Visitors* Paul Mason
(A&C Black, 2009)
A clear look at some famous UFO
cases and whether they are genuine
or hoaxes. This book also has bright
graphic explanations of the basic
science of UFOlogy.

UFOs: Are They Real? David Orme
(Ransom Publishing, 2006)
A combination of a fictional story
with nonfiction text, this book is sure
to grab your attention and keep it
till you get to the last page.

Aliens and UFOs Christopher Evans
(Carlton Books, 2008)
By an award-winning science-fiction
writer, this book takes readers on
an unbelievable journey into the
world of unexplained UFO and alien
encounters.

Although the following are adult
titles, they would be useful to
confident readers who want to find
out more:
*The Mammoth Encyclopedia of
Extraterrestrial Encounters*
Ronald D. Story (editor)
(Robinson, 2002)
*UFOs: A History of Alien Activity
from Sightings to Abductions to
Global Threat* Rupert Matthews
(Arcturus Publishing, 2009)

The Internet

The Internet can be a minefield for
alien hunters—there are a lot of
fakers and hoaxers out there. Some
sites are good, though, including:

www.ufocasebook.com/
Contains vast amounts of
information on UFOs and aliens.
Among the most interesting things
are the photos, including many
allegedly showing aliens.

**www.ufoevidence.org/cases/
ufocaseshome.asp**
One section of a huge site, which
allows you to look at UFO reports by
decade or by region.

Movies and DVDs

E.T. (1982, director Steven Spielberg)
A classic, this story of how a group of
children try to send a lost alien home
is sure to make you laugh AND cry.

Men in Black I & II (1997 & 2002,
director Barry Sonnenfeld)
Funny, sci-fi adventure movies about
two men trying to save the world
from aliens who want to blow it up.

Note to parents and teachers: every effort
has been made by the Publishers to ensure
that these web sites are suitable for children,
that they are of the highest educational
value, and that they contain no inappropriate
or offensive material. However, because of
the nature of the Internet, it is impossible to
guarantee that the contents of these sites
will not be altered. We strongly advise that
Internet access is supervised by a responsible
adult.

index

Alien/Aliens 27, 29
Area 51 18, 19
Australia 12, 13

Belgium 14, 15, 17
Brazil 20, 21

China 24, 25
Close Encounters of the
   Third Kind 10, 11

District 9 27, 28, 29

E.T. 26, 27

fakes 4, 19

Flatwoods Monster 8–9,
   29
foo fighters 6–7

Grays 28

hoaxes 17
humanoids 8, 17

Knowles (family) 12, 13

Las Lomas UFO hoax 17

Men in Black 27
meteors 9, 25
Mexico 16–17

mother ships 17, 21
Mothman 29
movies 5, 10, 26–27

Predator 27

The War of the Worlds
   26
tornado 13

United States 8, 9, 10,
   11, 18, 19, 22, 23, 29

Wells, H.G. 26
Westendorff, Haroldo,
   20, 21
World War II 7

This edition first published in 2012 by

Sea-to-Sea Publications
Distributed by Black Rabbit Books
P.O. Box 3263, Mankato, Minnesota 56002

Copyright © Sea-to-Sea Publications 2012

Printed in China

All rights reserved.

9 8 7 6 5 4 3 2

Published by arrangement with the
Watts Publishing Group Ltd, London.

Series editor: Adrian Cole
Art director: Jonathan Hair
Design: Mayer Media
Picture research: Diana Morris

A CIP catalog record for this book
is available from the Library of Congress.

ISBN: 978-1-59771-315-3

February 2011
RD/6000006415/001

Acknowledgements:
Alperium/Shutterstock: 5br, 9tr, 23b inset, 25c, 29br. Steve
Back/Daily Mail/Rex Features: 19b. dbarkertv.com/still from
The Edge of Reality : 22b. Janet & Colin Bord/Forteanpix: 1,
8b, 29tr. Jackie Carvey/Shutterstock: 2. CC: 15br, 17br, 25t.
Cody Images: 23b. Richard Cooke/Alamy: 20c. Columbia/AF
Archive/Alamy: 10b. Columbia/Kobal Collection: 11t, 27c.
Dale O'Dell/Alamy: 21b. Mary Evans PL/Alamy: 7t, 16b.
Everett Collection/Rex Features: 5bl. Markus Gann/
Shutterstock: 11b, 15bl, 17bl, 19t, 21t, 27t, 27b.
Alistair Heap/Alamy: 14b. Gerrit de Hens/Alamy: 18.
Insadio Photography/Alamy: 12b. Natalia Lukiyanova/frenta/
Shutterstock: 3. Moviestore Collection/Alamy: 28b.
Ocean/Corbis: 9. Willoughby Owen/Flickr/Getty Images: 13b.
Lee Pettet/istockphoto: 4tl, 8tl, 12tl, 16tl, 20tl, 24tl, 28tl, 28tr.
Chip Simons/Getty Images: 4b. Nathan Smith/istockphoto:
front cover. Universal/Kobal Collection: 26b.
Charles Walker/Topfoto: 6b. Zhou chun/ImagineChina: 24b.

Every attempt has been made to clear copyright.
Should there be any inadvertent omission please
apply to the publisher for rectification.